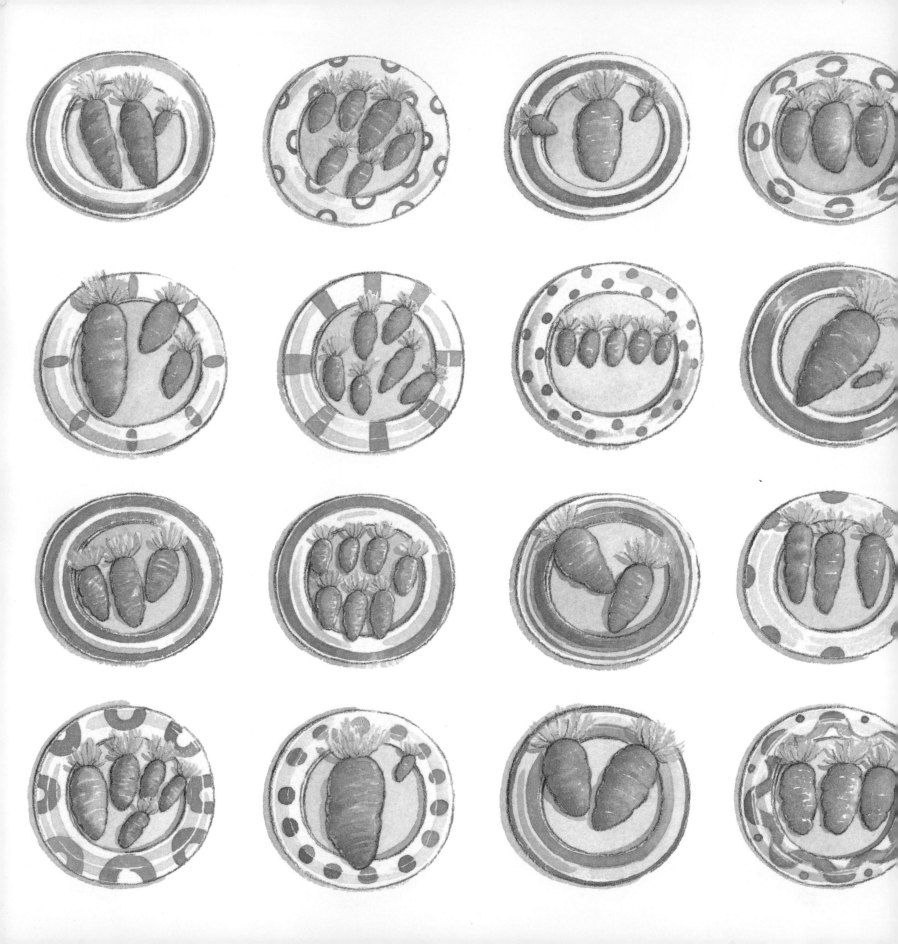

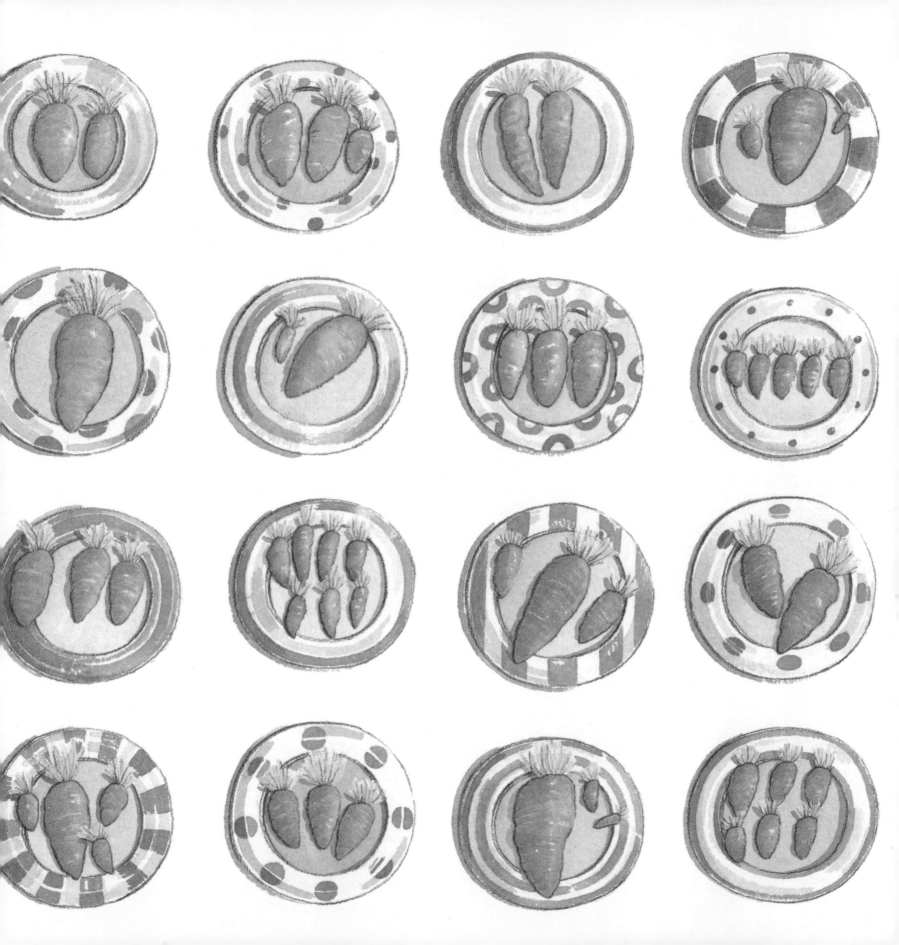

For
Aaron
and Zoë

PUFFIN BOOKS
Published by the Penguin
Group: London, New York,
Ireland, Australia, Canada,
India, New Zealand
and South Africa

Penguin Books Ltd,
Registered Offices:
80 Strand, London
WC2R 0RL, England

penguin.com
First published 2006
Published in this
edition 2007

1 3 5 7 9 10 8 6 4 2

Text and illustrations
copyright ©
Penny Ives, 2006

The moral right of the
author/illustrator has
been asserted

Manufactured
in China

ISBN 978–0–140–56988–9

Rabbit Pie

By PENNY
IVES

PUFFIN

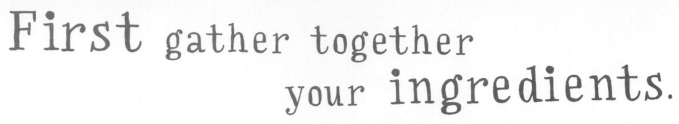

First gather together
your ingredients.
One game of hide-and-seek
One bath
Six pairs of pyjamas
Six cups of milk
One story
A sprinkling of soft kisses
Six large carrots

Then
find
six
small
rabbits ...

... if
you
can!

Take off any
dirty
bits . . .

. . . and place in warm **soapy** water.

Gently scrub.

Watch **very** closely.

Fold
into a
soft
towel

and allow to **cool** down.

Pat dry,
dust
the bottoms

and **lightly**
brush
the tops.

Slowly pour in

six
cups
of milk.

Tuck in,
sprinkling
with
kisses.

Leave in a **warm** place until morning.

When quite ready, serve with **fresh** carrots.

Sweet
Rabbit
Pie!

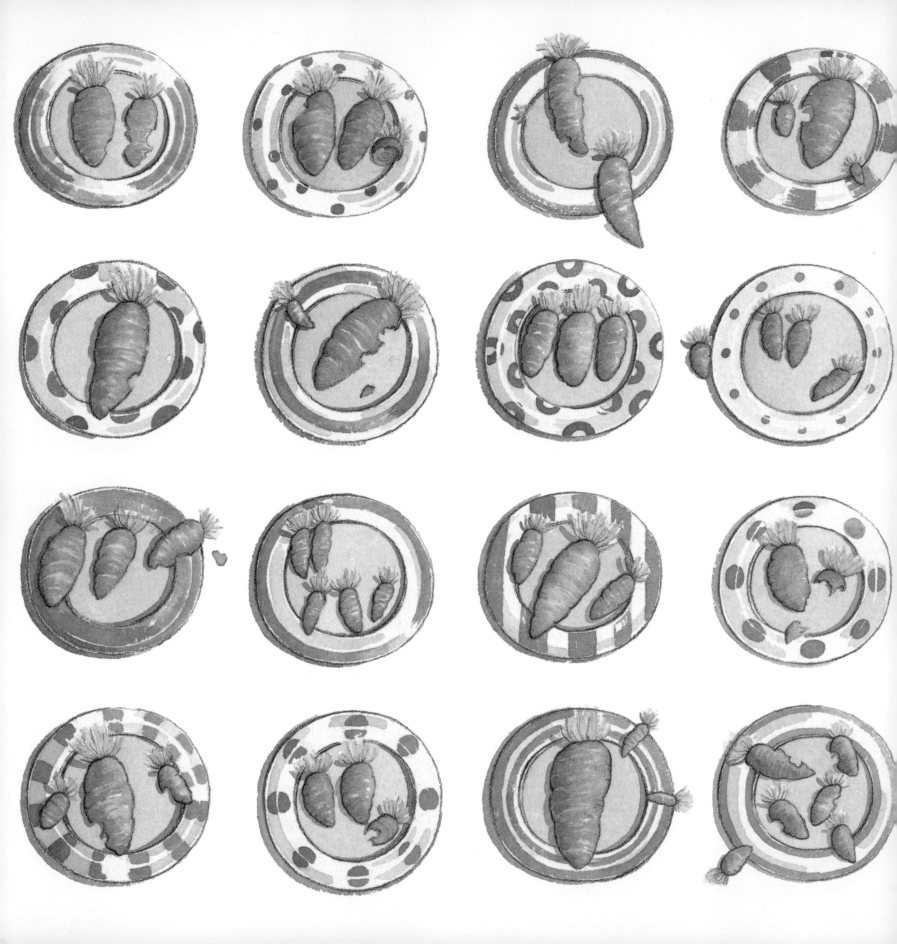

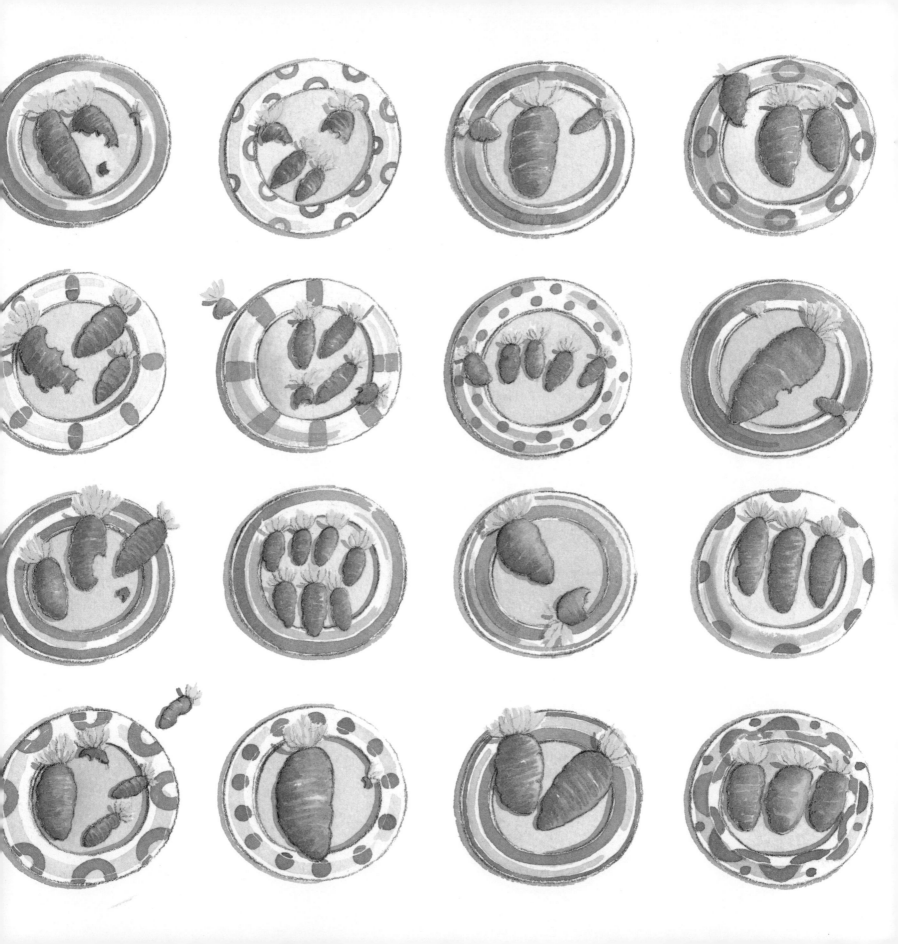